To Barbara Firth
M.W.

❧

To Morwenna
B.F.

First published 2007 by Walker Books Ltd
87 Vauxhall Walk, London SE11 5HJ

2 4 6 8 10 9 7 5 3 1

Text © 2007 Martin Waddell
Illustrations © 2007 Barbara Firth

This book has been typeset in Golden Cockerell

Printed in Singapore

British Library Cataloguing in Publication Data:
a catalogue record for this book is available from the British Library

ISBN 978-1-84428-541-9 (HB)
ISBN 978-1-4063-0863-1 (PB)

www.walkerbooks.co.uk

Bee Frog

Martin Waddell   Barbara Firth

WALKER BOOKS
AND SUBSIDIARIES

LONDON · BOSTON · SYDNEY · AUCKLAND

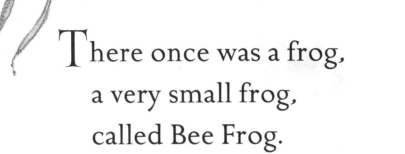

There once was a frog,
a very small frog,
called Bee Frog.

Bee played all day with her sisters and brothers.
They played
Can't Catch Me, Frog,
Frog-Hop and
Frog-Plop and ...

I'm Not a Frog,
I'm a
DRAGON.

Then Mum Frog called them in.

"I'm Bee Frog the Dragon,"
Bee told Mum Frog.
"Yes, Bee, that's nice,"
croaked Mum Frog.

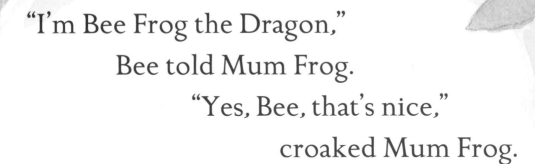

"I'm not nice, I'm a dragon," croaked Bee.
"Yes, dear, I see," croaked Mum Frog.

"I'm Bee Dragon,"
Bee told Dad Frog.
"Be quiet, Bee,"
croaked Dad Frog.

"I'm a very fierce dragon!" croaked Bee.
"So I see," said Dad Frog, without looking at Bee.

"I'm Bee Dragon,"
Bee told Grandma Frog.
But Grandma Frog was fast asleep on her lily
and she didn't hear Bee.

"No one listens to me!"
croaked Bee Frog.

"I'm hopping off!"
croaked Bee Frog.

"I'm hopping off
        and I'm not coming back,

not ever,
      not *never!*"

hop

hop

hop

hop

hop

hop

hop

Bee Frog landed on a dark stone,
with reeds all around it.

This is good! thought Bee Frog.
I like it! thought Bee.
I love it! thought Bee.

And she made dragon noises
all by herself.

I'm Bee Dragon! thought Bee.

I'm Bee Dragon, the really fierce dragon! thought Bee.

Everyone's SCARED of Bee Dragon!

thought Bee.

Then ...

I wonder if dragons get lonely? thought Bee.

Mum and Dad Frog
came looking for Bee.
"Bee Dragon! Bee Dragon!"
they croaked.

Bee sat very still, until they
were almost beside her.
And then ...

CROAK!

Bee ambushed her mummy and daddy.

"We've found you,
   Bee Dragon!"
   croaked Mum and Dad Frog.

"I'm not really a dragon,"
   croaked Bee.

"Well..."
   croaked Mum Frog.

"You look like a very
   fierce dragon to me!"
   said Dad Frog.

"I'm not! I'm your BEE!"
   croaked Bee Frog.

And they all hopped off
home for frog tea.